Be My Valentine

by M.J. Carr
illustrated by Katy Bratun

SCHOLASTIC INC.

New York Toronto London Auckland Sydney

For Jessie and Gea
— M.J.C.
To Alma Bratun, with love
— K.B.

ISBN 0-590-45131-6

Copyright © 1992 by Jan Carr.
Illustrations copyright © 1992 by Katy Bratun.
All rights reserved. Published by Scholastic Inc.

12 11 10 9 8 7   4 5 6 7/9

Printed in the U.S.A.   24
First Scholastic printing, January 1992

It was the eve of Valentine's Day. Even the moon
was celebrating.

But inside the coffee shop, it was a night like any other. The mice were huddled in the storeroom, listening for the final click of the key in the restaurant door. That would be their signal that the last waiter had gone home and their own work could begin.

One mouse was missing. Isadore. He was crouched in a quiet corner, working on his poem.

"You're softer than a porcupine.

Athena, be my valentine."

"I just can't get it right!" he wailed. He tore up the poem and tossed the pieces into the air. More than anything, Isadore wanted Athena to be his valentine. If only he could find the courage to tell her!

Athena. She could run faster than any mouse,
boy or girl.

She could scale table legs with ease.
   Every night, without fear, she leapt from counter stool to counter stool.

And she always managed to bring back, clenched between her pointed, pearly teeth, the biggest chunk of food of all.

"Eyes as bright as polished chrome," wrote Isadore. "A smile as saucy as ketchup."

"Oh, what's the use?" he moaned. "It's all been said before."

He crumpled up his poem as if it were yesterday's menu and aimed it for the trash.

"Hey, Izzy, old buddy, old pal!" It was Cosmo, Isadore's best friend. "Why so down at the whiskers? Inkwell run dry?" Cosmo caught the poem midair and slapped Isadore on the back.

"Izzy, Izzy, Izzy. You've got to talk to her.
It's now or never! Come on!"
   Cosmo shoved Isadore up to Athena.
Athena smiled. Isadore held out the poem.

But right at that moment, the key clicked in its lock.

"Let's go!" Athena cried, signaling the others.

The mice were off and running. The poem fell to the floor.

"Athena!" Isadore ran after her. All around him mice were scurrying hither and thither, gathering food. "Athena!"

"Athena, I've got this . . ."

A crust of a grilled cheese sandwich whizzed past his head.

". . . poem that I want to . . ."

The corner of a cherry Danish narrowly missed his ear.

The pile of food grew high. Isadore was trapped.

The last mouse back was Athena. In her claws she
held a whole half a BLT, fallen off someone's plate and
overlooked by the waiter's broom. Isadore poked his
head out from behind the pile.

"Izzy!" cried Athena. "I was wondering where you
were. I was hoping we could . . ."

"Ketchup," stammered Isadore. Athena looked at
him strangely. "Polished chrome," he tried again.

His poem didn't seem to be working. Athena
scampered away.

"I knew it!" cried Isadore. "She doesn't want to be my valentine."

"But Izzy, you didn't even ask her if . . ."

"She doesn't believe me!"

"You didn't even tell her that you . . ."

"Cosmo, I don't have all night to stand here and
talk to you! I've got work to do! There's *got* to be
a way to prove to her I really want to be friends!"
    Time was running low.

Isadore stayed up half the night working on a new poem. Then he stayed up the other half memorizing it.

"I'd swim the widest fountain," he read out loud. "Climb the highest mountain."

The morning sun cast its still-sleepy light across the paper. Valentine's Day was dawning. Isadore had a plan.

That night, Valentine's night, as the mice spilled
into the coffee shop, Isadore was first in line. He
scrambled up to the top of the counter.

"Athena!" he called. She looked up. "Watch me!"

Isadore dove into the long tray underneath the
fountain and swam through the sticky, sweet soda
to the other side.

Then he scrambled over the edge, clambered up
past the summit of Mount Olympus, and higher
to the top of the cake stand.

He shook himself dry and cleared his throat to recite his poem. He opened his mouth. Nothing came out.

"Izzy?" Athena called up to him. "What in the world are you doing up there?"

At the sound of her voice, Isadore lost his balance. He tumbled off the cake stand, smack onto the counter.

The coffee shop fell silent. Not a mouse squeaked. All the mice in the restaurant were staring up at Isadore. He'd made a fool of himself. In front of everyone.

Valentine's Day was a disaster.

Isadore slowly picked himself up. In front of him, next to the cash register, was a small bowl of candy hearts. On each heart was printed a little saying. Isadore picked one out of the bowl. He handed it to Athena. "Be my valentine," it said simply.

"Oh, Izzy!" cried Athena. "All along I've been hoping
we could be valentines!"

"Really? You mean you have?"

Athena twined her tail in his. Isadore grinned.

"New friend! True friend! Happy end!" he crowed.

Cosmo scuttled by, a soggy french fry in his mouth.
"Race you to the pickle pot!" said Isadore.

Athena leapt across the wide aisle to the booth beyond. Isadore was close on her tail.